Adapted by Nancy E. Krulik
From the screenplay by Christian Ford and Roger Soffer
And story by Paul M. Glaser

INTERSCOPE COMMUNICATIONS Presents
In Association with POLYGRAM FILMED ENTERTAINMENT
A film by PAUL M. GLASER
SHAQUILLE O'NEAL   "KAZAAM"   FRANCIS CAPRA
Executive Producers TED FIELD   LEONARD ARMATO   ROBERT W. CORT
Co-Executive Producers SHAQUILLE O'NEAL   BRUCE BINKOW   BETH JELIN
Screenplay By CHRISTIAN FORD & ROGER SOFFER
Story By PAUL M. GLASER
Produced By SCOTT KROOPF PAUL M. GLASER and BOB ENGELMAN
Directed By PAUL M. GLASER
© 1996 INTERSCOPE COMMUNICATIONS, INC.
Credits not contractual

ISBN 0-590-93103-2

12 11 10 9 8 7 6 5 4 3   6 7 8 9/9 01/0
Printed in the U.S.A.   24
First Scholastic printing, July 1996

SCHOLASTIC INC.
New York   Toronto   London   Auckland   Sydney

1

Max Connor took a quick look over his shoulder. Darn! The gang of older boys was gaining on him. Why can't they leave me alone? Max wondered as he pedaled faster on his bicycle.

Max dropped his bike beside an abandoned building and ran inside. Maybe the gang would ride right past him.

No such luck. The bigger boys charged into the building after Max. At first they couldn't figure out where Max had gone. Then they heard a loud crash, followed by Max's screams!

Max looked around the damp, dingy basement of the abandoned building. He'd tumbled straight through the floorboards!

Clunk. Max's hand accidentally banged against an old metal boom box that was buried deep in the trash. Thump, thump, thump. Music started blaring from the box. The song was in a language Max had never heard before.

Max tried frantically to quiet the box. But it was too late. The gang of boys was on its way to the basement.

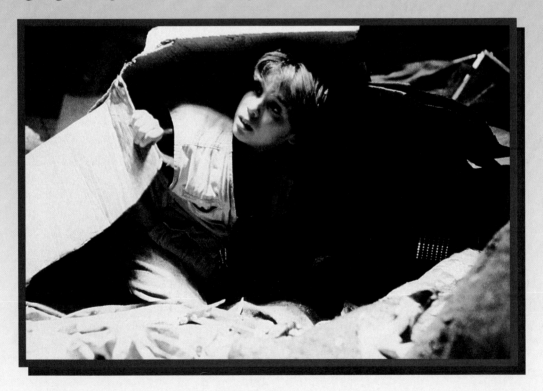

One of the big kids grabbed Max's arm, pulling him to his feet. Max's foot brushed against the boom box's eject button. Suddenly a wild whirling wind began to blow from the box.

The boys looked up in fear. There before them stood the largest man they'd ever seen. And he was dressed strangely, too.

"WHO DARE TO WAKE ME?" the man bellowed.

Suddenly the gang members weren't so brave. They shot out of the building, leaving Max to face the giant alone.

Max tried to make a run for it, but the huge man kneeled before him, blocking his path. "Hey, don't you turn your back on me," the man said to a rap beat. "I'm a man of the ages. Straight out of the pages. I'm outrageous. You can't contain this. I AM KAZAAM!

"Where do you think you're going?" Kazaam asked. "Make your three wishes, and I'm outta here. Do you realize who I am? I'm your genie."

Max looked down at Kazaam. Was this guy nuts, or what?

There was only one way to get rid of the guy. Max had to make a wish. "All right," he said. "Gimme a car. Jaguar. Black XKE."

Kazaam cracked his knuckles, shook his head, and bellowed, "I AM KAZAAM!" Then he flung his hands wildly. Electricity flew from his ears. Magical sparks dashed from his fingertips. And then . . . nothing happened.

"Great try. Keep in touch, okay?" Max said sarcastically as he got on his bike and pedaled toward home.

The next morning, Max rolled sleepily out of bed and went to the kitchen. But instead of his mother, Max found a note. "Had to cover Brenda's shift. Be back for dinner. Love, Mom."

There was something else on the table, too. Signed divorce papers from Max's dad, Nick. Max hadn't seen him in ten years. Max looked at the return address on the envelope and headed out the door. He wasn't going to school. He was taking a bus trip downtown — to find his dad.

The bus left Max a few blocks from the address on the envelope. While he was looking for a street sign, he saw . . . Kazaam! Quickly, Max turned and walked in the other direction.

Kazaam leaped in front of the boy. "Uh, back there, your first wish. That could happen to any genie. I was a little rusty."

"Why don't you leave me alone?" Max asked.

"Look! You called me into this world. So wish. Wish for a castle. Wish for a faster chariot," Kazaam replied.

"Come on, boy, just give it a try." Kazaam started to rap.

"I wish I had junk food, from here to the sky," Max rapped back.

Kazaam waved his hands and said the magic words.

"I AM KAZAAM!"

Plop! A cheeseburger landed on Max's head. "That's it? A burger?" Max snickered.

Crash! There was a crack of thunder. And before Max knew it, hamburgers, burritos, chocolate bars, and jelly beans rained from the skies. No doubt about it, Max had to believe in Kazaam now.

The return address on his father's envelope led Kazaam and Max to a nightclub called the Music Boxx. Max walked inside and searched until he found an office with the name NICK MATTEO on the door. Max stared through the glass.

"What are you doing here?" Nick bellowed from behind his desk. "Who let this kid in? What is this — an amusement park?" he asked his staff. Then he turned to Max. "What's your name, kid?"

"Maxwell," Max answered. "Maxwell Connor."

Nick gazed at the boy. "You're . . . my . . . son," Nick said slowly.

Nick turned to the other people in his office. "Everybody, this is my boy, Maxwell," he explained. Suddenly the door flew open. In walked Kazaam disguised as a pizza delivery man! Everyone stared at him in amazement. Everyone except Max, that is.

"Three large, two medium, Pizza Zam's here to bust the tedium," he said. Max smiled. What a perfect day — his favorite food, and the chance to see his dad. Then Nick handed him passes for a Spinderella and KEI rap show. The perfect day had just gotten better.

That night, Max snuck out of his room and headed off to the club. Kazaam went along, dressed like a rapper. But no matter how he's dressed, a seven-foot genie always stands out in a crowd. Even Spinderella and KEI noticed him!

"You come to gawk or you come to jam it?" Spinderella challenged Kazaam.

"I am Kazaam," he rapped. "I'm more than I seem. You all are looking at your dream!"

While Kazaam was enjoying his newfound stardom, Max headed back to his dad's office. As he reached the door, Max heard two men talking. "Lemme paint you a picture," Nick was saying angrily to a sound engineer named Ed. "I got fifty thousand blank tapes showing up on a loading dock. So you will have that live Spinderella and KEI tape ready by three a.m.!"

Max was shocked. His father was asking a sound engineer to make an illegal tape of the concert. His dad could go to jail!

Max left the club and walked nervously down the alleyway.

"What are you doing here?" a familiar voice asked. Max looked up in fear. He was surrounded by the gang of older boys from school.

Max pointed toward the club. "I was in there, okay? I was in the VIP section. I can go anywhere I want," Max bragged.

But the boys didn't believe him. "I'm telling the truth!" Max insisted. "They're doing a live recording right now. I could put the tape in your hands."

The gang's leader put his hand squarely on Max's shoulder. "You mean that, homie?" he said.

Max needed Kazaam's help. But Kazaam was off celebrating his slammin', rapping success with Nick's boss, Malik.

Kazaam didn't know that Malik was dangerous. Or that he was the man Nick was making illegal tapes for. All Kazaam knew was that Malik served good snacks.

Malik offered Kazaam a brass bowl filled with things that looked like marbles.

"Nubian goat eyes?" the genie asked excitedly.

Malik nodded slyly. There was definitely something more to this giant rapper than met the eye.

As Kazaam snacked on goat eyes, Max led the gang to the loading dock behind the Music Boxx. They waited in the shadows as Nick gave some truckers a huge wad of money. Then Ed, the sound engineer, emerged from the building, holding a cassette in his hand.

Two of the gang members jumped Ed! They wrestled the cassette from his hands and ran off into the night. Max followed close behind.

The next morning, Max woke up to Kazaam's voice. The big guy was rapping in his sleep!

Max brained the sleeping genie with a baseball. Kazaam woke with a start, but smiled.

"You know you were right to get me out there last night," Kazaam thanked Max. "They loved me. Malik said I've got a future in the rap biz! He even gave me a chance to rap at the club tonight! You and your dad have a nice night?"

Max groaned. Nice night? Sure. If you call finding out that your dad's involved in illegal activities "nice."

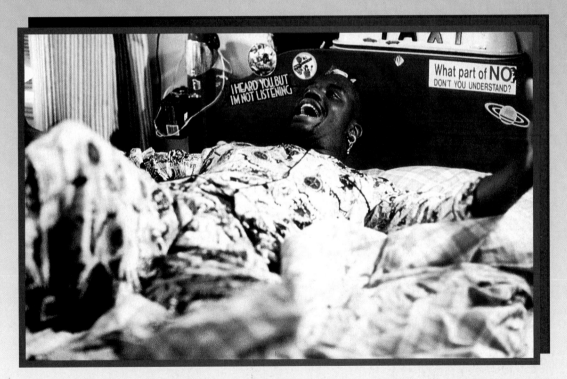

Later that morning, Kazaam walked Max to school. "Man, it must be great to be a genie," Max said. "You can just snap your fingers and have anything."

Kazaam shook his head. "Can't make myself free."

"I wish I could change things," Max thought out loud.

"You're not talking about genies," Kazaam said. "You're talking about a Djinn. A Djinn is free. A Djinn can do anything. Love, change the future, change people's fates." Kazaam looked sadly at Max. "But Djinns exist only in fairy tales," he said.

"I don't believe in fairy tales," Max told his genie. "But then again, I didn't believe in three wishes."

Kazaam grinned. "And look what you got!"

Max stared at his watch. Yikes! He was late for school! "Oh, man! I'd better get going!" Max said as he dashed off.

Kazaam looked at his watch. He was late for rehearsal. "See ya!" the big guy called out as he headed toward the Music Boxx.

Max raced through the halls to his classroom. But before he could reach the door, the gang of boys surrounded him. Only this time, they seemed really happy to see him!

"So you gotta talk to your dad," one of the boys said. "Tell him if he wants the tape back, it's going to cost him."

The boys drew in closer to Max. They meant business.

Max nodded. He had no choice but to deliver the message to his dad.

Max hightailed it to the Music Boxx. He peered through a
crack in the door jamb of his father's office.

"You knew the tape was worth a million dollars," Max heard
Malik say with an eerie calmness.

"I'll find . . . the tape. . . . " Nick stuttered, sounding frightened.

"But what will I find?" Malik threatened. "My loyal friend, or a
man at the bottom of the lake?"

Max gulped. He had to get the tape back to his dad . . . and fast!

Max knew there was only one person who could help him get the tape. "Kazaam! Kazaam!" the boy cried out.

Kazaam was having lunch at a fancy restaurant. When he lifted his glass, he got a big surprise! There was Max, reflected in the water, crying out for help. Kazaam dropped the glass in shock.

"Hey!" Suddenly Max was sitting in the middle of the table, soaking wet, and surrounded by broken glass. "I gotta make a wish," he said as he dried himself with a cloth napkin. "I wish I had the master tape from last night's show."

With a flash of light, Max found himself back at the Music Boxx, Kazaam at his side.

"What are we doing here?" he asked the genie.

"Saving you a wish," Kazaam replied, riffling through a stack of tapes.

Max grabbed the genie's arm. "It's not here."

Kazaam looked into Max's eyes. "Why isn't it here?" he asked gently. "Talk to me, Max. I'm your buddy."

"I don't need a friend," Max barked. "I need a genie. Now grant my second wish."

Kazaam's face hardened. "Your wish is my command," he said slowly. "I AM KAZAAM!"

Late that afternoon, as Max was leaving school, a big Cadillac pulled up to the curb. Nick got out and guided his son into the car. "Max, we've got to talk," Nick said. "Never in my life have I seen anything so stupid. I know what you and your punk friends stole. I can't believe this, you're supposed to be ten years old."

"Twelve," Max corrected him. The boy looked sadly at the floor. His own father didn't even know how old he was!

Nick could see he'd hurt Max's feelings. "Max, you don't want to live my life," he said in a softer voice. "You have a choice, I don't. Guys like me can't pretend it didn't happen. There are no second chances in life."

Max dug into his backpack and pulled out the master tape from the concert. Nick took the tape and put it in his pocket.

There was nothing left to say. Max opened the car door, got out, and walked away.

Malik was already in Nick's office by the time Nick returned to the Music Boxx with the tape. Malik had been watching a video-tape taken by a security camera. And Malik liked what he saw. The tape was of Kazaam and Max. Malik smiled an evil grin as he watched Kazaam use his magic to get the Spinderella and KEI tape.

Malik's greedy eyes grew bright. It was just as Malik had thought. The big rapper was no man — he was a genie.

That night, the audience roared as Kazaam took the stage. "Hang on, I'm contagious! I'm outrageous! I am Kazaam!" he rapped.

Max waited for Kazaam to come backstage. "Kazaam, I want my last wish," the boy said. "I wish my dad had a second chance."

"No can do," Kazaam answered him. "I cannot do it. I can't snap my fingers and make you all happy. I'm not some Djinn."

"You just don't want to grant this third wish, do you?" Max accused the genie. "You're a star now, and you don't want to go back into your box!" The boy ran off in tears.

When Kazaam went back onstage for the second show, Malik stole the genie's boom box and carried it up to Nick's office. Nick, Max, and two strong bodyguards were waiting there for him.

"Max, I'll make you a deal," Malik said. "You make a wish that says I get your genie and everything my heart desires. If you try anything clever, your dear father will wake up dead!"

Then Nick sprang into action. He hit one of Malik's bodyguards. Then he and Max raced down the hall as two of Malik's goons chased after them. The thugs grabbed Nick, and forced Max to go to Malik's office.

"Now grant my wish," Malik ordered the boy.

"Kazaam is my genie," Max insisted, "and as long as I am standing here, he's gonna do what I tell him."

Malik shrugged. "Then I guess my only problem is you're still standing," he replied. With a wave of his hand, two large men carried Max away . . . permanently!

Kazaam had no idea anything was wrong with Max. He was busy rapping. Then, suddenly—poof!—Kazaam vanished from the stage in a flash of light.

He found himself standing before Malik. "It worked!" Malik said with glee. "Now be a good genie and get in the boom box! You have been called . . . by me! I'm your master."

Kazaam stared at Malik with determined eyes. "I'm never gonna be your slave."

Kazaam lifted Malik off the ground. "Where's Max!" he demanded.

"He fell down the elevator shaft," Malik said fearfully. "Please don't hurt me."

"Wish not granted!" Kazaam bellowed. He wadded Malik into a ball and slam-dunked him into a trash chute. Then he raced to Max.

Kazaam lifted the almost lifeless boy in his arms. "In five thousand years you are the only friend I ever had," Kazaam cried. "I just wish . . . I could grant your wish." His tears fell on Max and light began to swirl around them.

Suddenly Max's eyes fluttered open. Kazaam's own wish had come true! "I made a wish and granted it!" the genie said joyfully.

Kazaam's body began to whirl in a mass of atoms and molecules.

Max looked up at Kazaam. "You can't leave," he said. "You haven't granted my third wish."

"But I have," Kazaam grinned. "You asked for a second chance for your father." Kazaam's face began to glow.

Now Max understood. Kazaam was no longer a genie; no longer anyone's slave. "You're a — "

"Djinn!" Kazaam finished the sentence with joy. "I'm free!"

Max knew it was time to say good-bye to his friend.

A giant wind carried Max to safety. As he flew, he heard Kazaam's mighty voice.

"We Are All Free. The Power Is in Your Heart."